This book belongs to:

_____

_____

Contents

First published 2008 by Brown Watson
The Old Mill, 76 Fleckney Road,
Kibworth Beauchamp, Leic LE8 0HG

ISBN: 978 0 7097 1801 7

EARLY READERS

Three Read Along Stories

Stories by Gill Davies

Illustrations by:
Gill Guile, Stephen Holmes,
Jane Swift and Lawrie Taylor

Brown Watson
ENGLAND

FLYING HIGH

Henry the helicopter has been away on a long trip.

"Look," says Mr Pilot. "We are nearly there. Are you ready to land?"

"Hello," sings a little bird. "Welcome back home, Henry."

"It is so good to see you all," says Henry as he swoops down to land near the other planes.

Ben and Ava are going for a ride in Henry today. They are very excited.

Ben helps his sister to get inside and then Ava helps her brother to put on his seat belt.

"Are you all ready?" asks the Captain.

"Yes!" shout the children . . . and then off they go, up into the blue sky.

9

Soon they are really high up.

"I can see everything from up here," says Ben.

"I can see the sea and the birds and an island," shouts Ava.
"Isn't it wonderful to be flying up in the air?"

"Yes," agrees Ben. "Brilliant! This is the best day of my life – ever!"

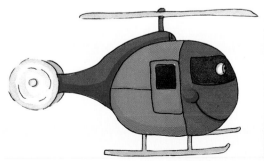

11

KEY WORDS

back	Mr
bird	put
brother	ready
children	sea
everything	see
get	sister
home	there
little	yes

WHAT CAN YOU SEE HERE?

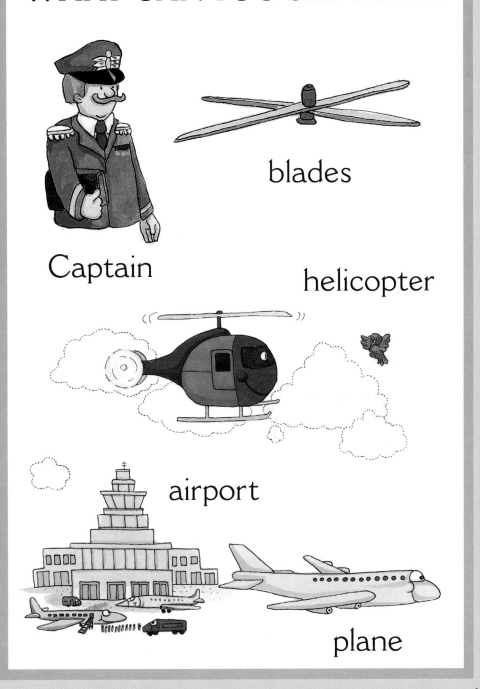

blades

Captain

helicopter

airport

plane

HOP AND SKIP

Alex and Olivia have two twin rabbits, Hop and Skip.

Hop is always very good. Skip is not always good. In fact, Skip is often a bit naughty. Sometimes she hides. Sometimes she skips away when Olivia opens the hutch door. Then poor Hop is sad.

"Oh dear, where is Skip today?" asks Olivia.
"Has she run away again?" asks Alex.

Olivia and Alex go to look for Skip.

"Have you seen her?" they ask Daddy. "No," says Daddy. He shakes his head. "Skip is such a naughty rabbit."

Suddenly Alex sees Skip. "There she is," he shouts. "She is hiding under the tractor."

"Come here, Skip!" calls Olivia. She holds out a piece of nice, sweet carrot. Skip hops over.

"Good girl, Skip!" says Olivia as she grabs Skip.

"Why did you run off again?" asks Alex. "Poor Hop is so sad when you go."

They take Skip back to her hutch.

Hop is so pleased to see Skip again . . . and Skip seems very pleased to see Hop too.

They rub noses and then eat all the carrot.

KEY WORDS

always	look
asks	nose
away	rabbit
come	run
Daddy	sad
have	seen
here	under
hops	where

WHAT CAN YOU SEE HERE?

tractor

hutch

rabbit

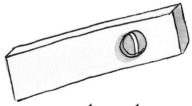

latch

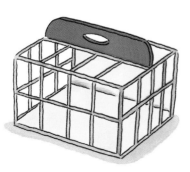

pet carrier

WHAT ABOUT ME?

Racer the rocking horse is very sad. It is his birthday and none of the other toys have remembered.

They all seem to be off in a hurry somewhere.

"What about me?" asks Racer as Daisy Doll rushes past in a car.

"What about me?" asks Racer as Blue Rabbit hurries into the dolls' house.

"What is going on?" asks Racer as two wooden puppets and Hot Dog run by, but they say nothing and run even faster.

"Oh dear," sobs Racer. "It is my birthday and no-one has remembered me."

He is very sad. He begins to cry.

He closes his eyes. Big round tears drip down his nose.

Then, suddenly, Racer hears a wonderful sound.

The toys have come out and are singing . . . They are singing, "Happy Birthday to You!" Racer is amazed.

"Here is a new blanket for you," says Daisy. "And we have hidden your cake and more presents from us in the dolls' house."

"Wow!" says Racer. "Thank you. What a brilliant surprise!"

KEY WORDS

about	me
car	new
dear	other
doll	round
from	thank you
his	toys
horse	us
into	what

WHAT CAN YOU SEE HERE?

dolls' house

puppets

rocking horse

blanket

friends

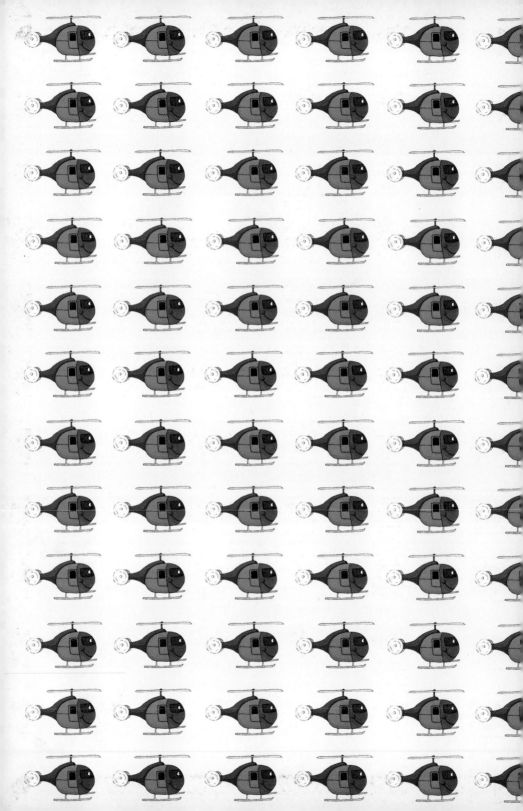